Sustah

and the

Annoying Sonnyboy

By: Sharon C. B. Hunter

Illustrated by: Derrick Thomas

Edited by: Claude R. Royston

BK Royston Publishing LLC

Jeffersonville, IN

BK Royston Publishing, Inc.

P. O. Box 4321

Jeffersonville, IN 47130

502-802-5385

www.bkroystonpublishing.com

Layout: BK Royston Publishing LLC

Illustrations by: Derrick J. Thomas

Cover Design by: Derrick J. Thomas

ISBN-13: 978-0692204177

ISBN-10: 0692204172

Printed in the United States of America

Dedication

This book is dedicated to Minister Mary Cummins, my deceased mother. Who shared so many funny stories of her childhood, hurts, triumphs, mischief, and fun? And to Ja'Leyha Chanel Mona'e , my great niece I called, "Boodles". I looked forward to play dates in the park, trips to the zoo, reading Sustahgirl to you and just watching you grow. However, God knows best! You both would have enjoyed the endless journeys of "Sustahgirl" fun! Please continue to watch over us all and help make Sustahgirl and the Annoying Sonnyboy a great success.

I love and miss you both so much!

Acknowledgements

I would like to acknowledge, my husband. You are so patient with me and listened to my ideas. You never told me I could not do it! You believed in me. I love you Sr. Pastor Dominic Hunter!

To my children, Danielle, Gabriel, Gwendalynn, Sharmaine, Phillip, and Jasmine. Thank you for listening to me read. Thank you for all your suggestions. Thank you for believing in me. Thank you for being my children. Words cannot express my love for you all.

To my entire family and church family, Tabernacle of Praise Christian Fellowship, you are all The Best, Loving, and God-fearing family. I love you for the prayers and pushing to chase my dreams!

And lastly, my publisher Julia, I know God sent you to me. This is a dream that has come true and I thank God for your patience, encouragement, and direction!

Introduction

The very first book I read as a child in its entirety was "The Lion, The Witch, and the Wardrobe" by C.S. Lewis. The fantasy world of Narnia had me hooked from the very first time Lucy entered the wardrobe and ended up in another world. I never forgot how it felt as I turned the pages and drifted into a totally different place and time. The sense of accomplishment I felt because I had read the whole book was also equally as memorable. Each time I picked up the book, I entered the wardrobe with Lucy, Edmund, Susan, and Peter in the world of Narnia. I believe in my heart after the completion of this read, I wanted to continue to read great books by C.S. Lewis and write!

The first book I wrote was for the Young Authors Club, and I continued to write poems, short stories.

You name it, I was writing. And as the years passed, I always dreamed of writing a children's book that captivated the imagination of the young reader, to make them think, and laugh all at the same time. Sustahgirl is the answer to that dream!

Sustahgirl was the nickname of my mother. She was the third of nine children, and the older of two girls. My mother was full of funny childhood stories that always had a deeper lesson around the funnies.

This first book from the Sustahgirl series tells the hilarious story of an orphaned cousin who comes to live with the Green family.

After Sonnyboy morns the death of his mother, the family rallies around him and decides he must live with Mother and Father Green. Sonnyboy gets along with all of Sustahgirl's brothers. He loves to prank and poke fun. However, his favorite person to aggravate is, Sustahgirl!

The fun is just beginning with the Sustahgirl book series. Read on and enjoy!

Table of Contents

CHAPTER ONE

I absolutely hate hospitals! They remind me of a haunted house because of all the sick people walking around. They look like zombies. I'm not trying to be mean but they scare me with the sick sounds they make. Even the machines are loud and make weird noises. All the doctors and nurses wear those strange white coats. They all pack around needles that remind me of a mini pocket Dracula that wants to suck your blood! They even talk in doctor language. It's like you are on another planet! It really freaks me out! I hide behind Mother when the doctors pass me in the hospital halls. I'm scared they are going to snatch me in a room and give me a shot. Another thing I hate about hospitals is the smell. It's especially gross! It smells like poop and bleach. It's disgusting! I don't even like the way they look.

All big and spooky on the outside, just like a haunted house! Even though I am scared of hospitals, I have to be strong because Mother's only sister, my Aunt Ruthie, is really sick. All of our family is going to pray for her today. Don't get me wrong, I don't mind praying for Aunt Ruthie or anybody. It's just that I am afraid of hospitals.

Today, not only is Mother taking Peewee and I, but she is taking all my brothers! This may not sound like a big deal but, Mother and Father have seven boys and two girls. People always say, "You have a really big family!" However, for us, it's just family. I love every one of my brothers but they can be some wild boys! So then, we rarely go anywhere in the same car or at the same time. Today is different and I want to know why!

Mother started out with a calm voice, "OK children, please go get in the van and get to your seat, so we can go to the hospital. I can't be late."

George led the pack running out the house. He looked like a rocket on two legs as he ran past Mother. The rest of my brothers followed him like a stampeding heard of cows down the front porch stairs.

George yelled, "I get to sit up front!"

Mother and I held Peewee's hand and walked down the steps, while Floyd leaped off the front porch and over the bushes. He shouted, "NO you are NOT sitting up front! I am the OLDEST and it's my turn."

After George and Floyd raced to the van, my other brothers joined in by pushing, shoving, and wrestling for the front seat. Mother and I continued to walk to the van when I turned and gave her a long sigh as I asked

"Mother, why are we all going to the hospital? You know how wild they can be sometimes. Did I do something wrong 'cause this is just cruel? "

While the boys were still wrestling at the van, Mother stopped in the front yard and gave me Peewee's hand. She twisted her face as she dug in her purse searching for her keys. Her normal calm voice turned into a loud voice that seemed to jump at my brothers as, "Stop push-ing and sho-ving." She then turned back to me still digging in her purse and answered quickly "No you didn't do anything wrong. Aunt Ruthie has taken a turn for the worse and I have to go to the hospital to see what is going on."

"Well, why didn't the boys ride with Father like they always do?" I asked.

Mother still shuffling and shaking her purse said,

"Your Father was already downtown, so he's going to meet us at the hospital."

My brothers were still fooling around when Mother found her keys. She stopped digging in her purse, and gave them "the face."

Now let me tell you about the face. When my mother gets really upset with anyone of us, she keeps her cool for a long time. But after she has had enough, she squishes her lips really tight. Then she presses her eyes together very small, and her nostrils flair like perfect little circles. When Mother gives us this face, she means business! And if you get "the face" and you keep acting out, she will get you good!

Mother's face was still squished up as she said very slowly, "nobody gets that front seat! Everybody gets in their assigned seat! Now get on that van, get those seat belts on, and when I come back you all better be ready to go!"

It's only when my mother gives "the face" that my brothers stop acting like wild boys! And since my brothers didn't want to get into trouble, they all started to get in the van, get seated and put their seatbelts on tight.

Now since we have a big family, Mother likes for everything to be very organized! So then, whenever we all travel together on our family van, she assigns seats.

6

Mother never fails to put one big kid between two little kids. Larry, Garry, and George climbed in the van first. The twins always manage to get into trouble. So then, Larry has to sit between Garry and George. They all sit on the front row because George is sneaky and Garry is just plain nasty. He always has a snotty nose. I think he likes to lick the snot. He is just gross and I can't be sitting by him! Larry, on the other hand, is always making up songs, and he is very talkative. We all love Larry, but his songs are silly and he talks too much! However, the twins do not seem to mind. My brother David can be mean to pretty much everybody. He wrestles, punches, and fusses but he loves caring for sick people and little kids. So then, Mother puts David between our baby sister PeeWee and Walter our baby brother. David is good with Peewee and Walter. He plays with Peewee and makes her laugh. He also answers Walter's thousand and one questions. Finally, Floyd, Jim, and I climbed to the back of the van.

By the way, my name is Mary Ethel Green but practically everybody in my whole family and church call me Sustahgurl! I used to be the only sister and the only girl until Peewee was born. So I picked up the nickname Sustahgurl. Floyd is the oldest and he always takes the window seat. So then, that leaves me in the middle and Jim on the end. I don't mind because Jim is my best brother.

Sometimes Mother will let the bigger boys walk to the store and get candy. I always want to go but Mother won't let me unless one of my brothers holds my hand. It makes me so mad because I don't need them to hold my hand. It doesn't matter anyway because none of them will do it, except Jim. I love them all, but he is the best. That's why I call him my best brother.

I held Peewee's hand and waited near the van while everybody was getting in their assigned seats. Mother walked over to the restaurant next door. She put up a sign on the front door that said, "CLOSED FOR THE DAY." And to be honest, it's a good thing we are closed cause my brothers were not being good at all. They can be so uncivilized.

I learned that word on our spelling list. It means my brothers are wild people! By the time Mother got back to the van, we were all in our assigned seats. We had our seat belts locked and ready to go. My mama doesn't play! She only asks you once before she gets you! And believe me, you are not going to like it if Mother has to "get you." She will give you more chores or take away your playtime. Sometime she takes away your treat. One time, she told George to pick up all the paper off the front yard, and he wouldn't do it. He just kept sneaking off and playing with his games. She got him real good. She made George stay with the babysitter for a whole week while she and Father took us all out for ice cream every day! For that whole week George had to watch us leave for the ice cream treat. He cried so hard. It was as if mother beat him with a bunch of wet switches. Although it didn't matter because he was right back to doing the same thing the very next day, getting into trouble!

Mother changes our van buddies every month. It is a good thing because my brother Floyd is going to make me hurt him. He knows I do not like to be teased, but he does it anyway. As soon as Mother started the van and drove off to the hospital, Floyd leaned over and whispered in my ear,

"Sonnyboy is going to be staying with us."

I shook my head real hard covered my ears and shouted back to Floyd, "Nope. NO. He is not!"

Floyd smiled and said, "Yep, it's true! Cause I overheard Mother talking to Uncle Jack. So let the pranks begin!"

He laughed with a ghoulish laugh like the TV vampires.

Even though my mother has a lot of brothers, she only has one sister, Aunt Ruthie, just like me. Well, Aunt Ruthie and Uncle Joe have only one son and his name is Clarence. We all call him Sonnyboy. You would think with a nick-name like that, he would be fun. But no, not Sonnyboy. He is not fun or at least not fun to me. He puts the "A" in annoying.

He is also nerve racking, bothersome, aggravating, basically, a pest! Sonnyboy's dad, Uncle Joe, died a long time ago. Therefore, Sonnyboy only has Aunt Ruthie and us, his family. He is the same age as my oldest brother Floyd. They both get along like two peas in a pod because they are always up to something. They like to team up and pick at all of us, laugh at us, or even make fun of us. However, Sonnyboy is the worst! As a matter of fact, he is worse than ants on a picnic! Before I could say another word, I began to remember the entire ratchet Sonnyboy antics from last summer.

He tossed worms in my face. He glued all my dolls together with crazy glue. One time we all were eating ice cream in the front yard. He jumped out from behind the big tree, pulled my ponytail and scared me half to death. I dropped my entire ice cream cone all over my brand new outfit. He just laughed and then all my brothers laughed too. Another time he saved stale water from the lake and made stinky balloon bombs. Every time he popped one of them things, it smelled like rotten eggs!

I believe he is friends with the devil because Uncle Jack says, "He's full of devilment."

Floyd is not quite as bad as Sonnyboy because he messes with you for a little while then he moves on to his next victim. However, Sonnyboy just won't quit! As soon as he sees me, he starts picking and pestering me. I think I am his favorite person to pick on. Sonnyboy has this big, gigantic smile. His teeth seem like they never end. He enjoys making my younger brothers and sister cry! He tries to make me cry but I am determined, it just won't happen! And anybody that knows Sustahgurl, knows when I make up my mind; I am going to do it! He will not make me cry! Even though I want to go see Aunt Ruthie, I need to know if Sonnyboy is going to be staying with us because he really bugs me!

Whenever Sonnyboy is around, my brothers' act like circus monkeys and Sonnyboy is their ringleader! They do whatever he says! They play the games that he wants to play. They laugh at all his dumb jokes. They have fart contest. They even go over to the lake where our whole family swims and have spitting contest. YUCK!

They are so gross!   When Sonnyboy is around they all do disgusting stuff. To sum it all up, Sonnyboy is annoying!

Now I'm not saying I don't get on anybody's nerves. I know I am not a perfect or a good girl all of the time. I sometimes get into things that my teacher says is mischief. I think she means I get into trouble. I don't start out looking for trouble. Trouble just finds me. But when Sonnyboy is around, trouble seems to find me quicker. Mother gives me 'the face' when I do these troublesome things. Father gives me a speech. I overheard Uncle Jack tell them, "That Sustahgurl is a hand- full."

 I think he means I stay into trouble. I don't go looking for trouble but when Sonnyboy is around, He causes that bad girl to come out of me and take over!

As Floyd was still making his weird vampire sounds, I scratched my head and leaned over to my other brother Jim and asked, "Is Sonnyboy really coming to stay with us?"

Jim waited to answer me because he was watching Mother in the rear view mirror. She has a rule, "no candy before dinner." But Jim loves to eat! So he saved some candy in his pocket that Father had given us.

As Mother turned down the dusty road to the hospital, Jim quickly popped his candy in his mouth and with a muffled voice said, "I don't know Sustahgurl. Ask Mother?"

I twisted my mouth and blew my hair out of my face and asked Jim another question, "Well, what do you think 'turn for the worse' means?"

Jim put his sticky, pudgy little fingers to his lips and said, "It probably means something bad cause worse is the opposite of good."

As we continued the drive to the creepy hospital, I leaned my head back on the seat and said to myself, 'I don't think this is going to be good.'

I sat quietly thinking about Aunt Ruthie. I just had to know what was going on, so I took Jim's advice and blurted out from my seat, "Mother what does 'turn for the worse' mean and where exactly is Sonnyboy?" Mother took a deep breath like she didn't want to give me the bad news and said, "Sustahgurl you might as well know, Sonnyboy is staying with Uncle Jack right now but he is going to be staying with us for a while or at least until Aunt Ruthie feels better.

Uncle Jack has seven girls and Sonnyboy needs to be around some boys."

I laid my head back on the seat and continued to talk with a whiny voice of fake concern. "Mama does he really have to come with us? Couldn't he keep staying with Uncle Jack or one of your other brothers? They don't have near as many children. I'm sure one more won't matter. Plus Uncle Jack probably wants a boy around. You know he has all those girls."

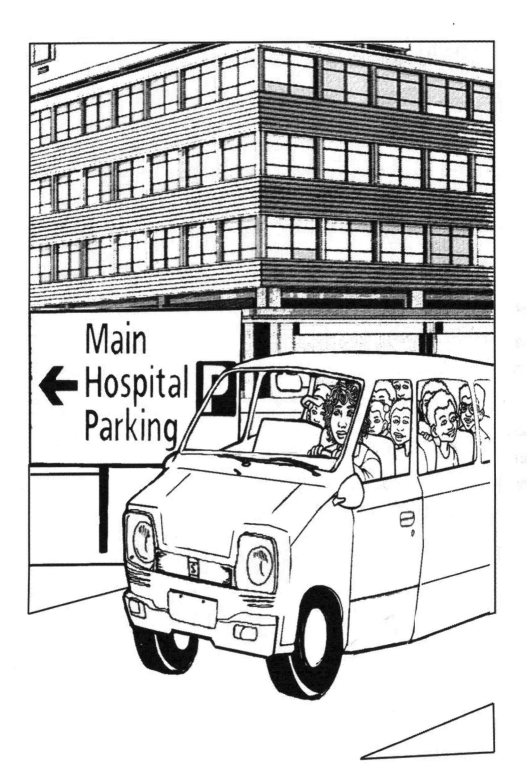

As Mother continued to drive the dusty road, she said, "Mary Ethel, we always want to do our best to do things God's way. We should always help family. We are all Sonnyboy's got. I hope that it won't be too long. So please honey be quiet and let's pray for Aunt Ruthie."

"Ok Mother I will pray. Now what does 'turn for the worse mean?" I asked.

"Mary Ethel," She said as if she was out of breathe again, "I have a lot on my mind right now. Please honey, Mother needs quiet."

As she tightened her hands on the steering wheel, she looked in the rear view mirror and gave me 'the face.'

It seems like I always get 'the face.' If she doesn't like my Christian attitude, I get 'the face.' If I'm getting on her nerves, she gives me 'the face.' Therefore, since I knew this face, I slumped back in my seat with my face of disappointment. Floyd suddenly leaned over toward me again and chanted his Sonnyboy cheer, "Sonnyboy is coming. Sonnyboy is coming! Sonnyboy is coming."

CHAPTER TWO

By the time we got to the hospital, my Mother's seven brothers were there with all there with their children.   My Family was everywhere.   All my little cousins were playing with the toys in the room. My bigger cousins were joking on one an-other and watching television. All of the adults were waiting for the doctors to come and tell us what was going on with Aunt Ruthie.   When one of our family members gets sick, we all try to come to the rescue. There are so many of us we look like a gang of cowboys riding in on horses with Bibles instead of guns. We try to help our sick family member to focus on other things be-sides being sick. Sometimes we sing. Sometimes we talk. Sometimes we laugh.   Other times we watch television and just keep them company, but we always, always, always, pray and ask God to bless them.

By now the entire family was at the hospital. We all pressed in the small waiting room and formed a circle. Uncle Jack is a very tall man. He has muscles that look like little barrels on his arms.

He is my mother's oldest brother so he usually leads the family prayers, but today he said, "Come on everybody, let's join hands with our family members and pray. I know that prayer changes things. I have seen it for myself. We are going to be in unity today as we pray for Ruthie. I know I usually pray the family prayers but today Lena is going to pray for Ruthie."

It is so funny to me when I hear people call my mothers first name, Lena. We all squeezed in the tiny, glass windowed room forming a double circle and holding hands.

I stood next to Mother and held her hand. By then, Father had gotten to the hospital and he stood on the other side of Mother. Uncle Jack nodded for Mother to pray after everyone was ready. She cleared her throat and prayed for Aunt Ruthie.

"Lord we thank you for your many blessings. Though we have a problem on today that we want to talk to you about. We must say thank you for all that you have done."

"No matter what happens you have blessed us to have a funny, helpful, loving sister, mother, aunt, cousin, because Lord she has been all these things. Please forgive us and we repent for focusing some days on the problems instead of the blessings you gave. You are mighty. Your works are mighty. We give Ruthie and her situation over to you and praise you before your will happens. Please heal Ruthie Lord but not our will but your will be done."

After Mother prayed everybody said, 'Amen' and it sounded like a thousand people. As everyone dropped hands and returned back to what they were doing, I hung around the adults and listened to them talk. I overheard one of my uncle's say, "I know God is in control, but it doesn't look good." Before I could squeeze back over to Mother's seat and question her about what my uncle said, the doctors finally came in the room wearing their weird white jackets.

They took Mother and all the adults to the room on the other side of the glass window. All the bigger children stopped looking at television and scrambled for a spot to watch through the window. We couldn't hear what the doctors were saying, but we all could see that the news was not good. I watched Father, through the window; hold Mother up as she cried. All my uncles tried to hold back their tears, but they could not.

They cried and kept saying that Aunt Ruthie went home. So then, I had figured out what 'a turn for the worse' meant. Aunt Ruthie died. As the adults came back in the small room with the children, they found a seat and continued to cry and wipe their tears. This made some of the smaller children cry. Sonnyboy was still seated with the rest of the kids near the window. He wasn't crying, but he looked scared and confused. After Father helped Mother to her seat, she said, "Sonnyboy come over here and sit next to Auntie. I want to talk to you."

She reached for him with her tissues and wet face. Sonnyboy got up from his seat, tucked his head, and shoved his hands in his pockets. He walked over to Mother and sat down in the seat next to her. When she told Sonnyboy his Mother had died, he burst into tears. I am so used to seeing him smiling and fooling around. It was strange to see him cry.   I didn't want Aunt Ruthie to die.   She always played with us in the summertime. We would play Marco Polo around the lake. She even camped out with us one night in our back yard.

Because my family is so huge, we can be very loud.   But nobody was talking today.   The room was so quiet. All you could hear was sniffles, moans, and tears. Sonnyboy balled up in the chair next to Mother. He tucked his head deep in the seat. His muffled cries filled the room. He cried so long that Uncle Jack came over and picked him up. Sonnyboy just lay on Uncle Jack and continued to cry on his shoulder.

I wanted to help him but I didn't know what to do. So I went over to the spot where my Mother was seated and sat down on the floor next to her and wrapped my arms around her feet.

As I continued to sit at Mother's feet, Uncle Jack's youngest daughter, Candice, toddled over and sat next to me. Candice is only five and really talkative. I don't think she really understood that Aunt Ruthie died. She has really bad allergies. Most of the time when she talks she has a stuffy, runny, red nose. So you really have to listen hard to what she says. Candice whispered, "Tusdagurl, my daddy said, Dunnyboy going be living with cha'll."

"I know Candice." I puffed my face and sighed.

"Tusdagurl, you know Dunnyboy is gonna be picking on ebbibody. "

I puffed my face bigger and held my words with another long sigh and said, "I know Candice."

"Tusdagurl did you know that he pulls me and my tusta's ponytails, and he locked me in the closet one time."

As Candice gave me more unwanted information, I could only say, "Yes, Candice I know."

"Well I was just telling you, Tudahgurl cause I'm glad he gonna be living wit 'chall cause he get on my nerbs."

I glared at Candice as she got up and toddled back across the hospital waiting room. Even though I didn't know all the words she said. I heard enough to know she was right! Although my cousin likes to drive me nuts, his father and mother were gone. I can't help but feel bad for him. Sonnyboy needed us more than ever, and we are his family! So Mother was right, we needed to give him a place to stay because Aunt Ruthie took a turn for the worse. She died. My whole family was sad including me. I really didn't know what to think except three things. Our family of eleven just got to number twelve. I am hungry! And what's going to happen to Sonnyboy?

CHAPTER THREE

There are much bigger Counties in Alabama, but Limestone County is not one of them. It is a small county! So by the time we got back home, everybody knew Aunt Ruthie died. Since my parents own the only soul food restaurant in Limestone County, the customers and our church family had gotten together to fix our whole family dinner. This is something that our community does. Mother says it's called hospitality, but I think it is because we love one another. It seemed like the whole church and community brought all kinds of food to the house. We had enough food to last at least two days straight. There were all kinds of food from pork chops to pies.

Oh yeah, the name of our family restaurant, KIN FOLK. Father says, 'In God's way, we are all His children, so that makes us all, KIN FOLK.' That's why he named our family restaurant, KIN FOLK.

You can order all your favorite soul foods like sweet ham, red sauce meatloaf, brown gravy meatloaf, hot fish, greens, green bean, sweet potatoes, mashed potatoes, macaroni and cheese, chess pies and chocolate cake. I love chocolate cake! My family can cook! Our food is delicious.

Mr. Jackson and Mr. Gonzales are two of the KIN FOLK restaurant regulars.

Mr. Jackson has the voice of a tuba, very deep and low. Mr. Gonzales has the voice that squawks like a chicken, if it could talk, of course. They come to the restaurant nearly every day. They like to sit at the high counter in front of the big window. They both are so smart. They always talk about the Bible, people, politics, and how the world is coming to an end, you know stuff like that. Mr. Jackson is a very big and tall man. He always orders, a bowl of greens with fat meat, cornbread, and a cup of black coffee. And guess what he brought to the house, greens and fat meat.

You may not know what fat meat is, it looks like a big fat piece of bacon but greasier. Another customer that is a regular at the restaurant is Ms. Flora. She brought meatloaf and chess pies. Next to my Mother and Uncle Jack, Ms. Flora is the greatest cook there ever was. She's a real sweet lady but Aunt Ruthie used to say she was the community gossip lady. She likes to talk about people. It does seem like she knows everything that goes on in the world. Well at least in the world of Limestone County.

One time she even knew that my brother, Floyd had a fight with one of the kids that lived two counties over. She told mother and Mother drove to get Floyd in her housecoat and slippers. How embarrassing. Though she talks a lot, she is a sweet lady. Ms. Flora has been really trying to help Mother.

"Lena, you just need to sit down and relax yourself. This has been a rough day. I will tend to everything," Ms. Flora said, as she led Mother to her big chair.

Mother said, "Flora, I can't have you moving all about in my house. You are my guest."

"Well, today I am not your guest. I am just a concerned friend trying to help. So please sit down and don't make me be ugly." She and mother chuckled as mother sat down in her big chair. I didn't want to leave my Mother's side. So I came over and sat next to her again. Although Mother was acting all strong, I knew she was really brokenhearted. All my uncles, aunts, cousins and folks like that, sat in the family room with Mother, eating and talking about Aunt Ruthie.

Mr. Jackson in his tuba voice said, "Lena, I know you gonna miss your sister. I can't help but remember her being such a prankster at the restaurant. She kept things lively. Do you remember that time when we were at the restaurant and she hid behind that door? She jumped out and scared little Jim to death? That child jumped so hard, he looked like he got stuck for a few minutes, and then when he did move, bread went all over the place!" He belly laughed.

"Yes, Mr. Jackson. My sister was a bit of a prankster. Her son Clarence is going to be staying with us for a while and he has that same playfulness" said Mother.

I jumped up and shouted, "Playfulness!"

All the adults looked at me like I had three heads and ten horns. See, where I come from children don't get into grown folks' conversation. As a matter of fact, Mother says adults have adult conversations and children have children's conversation. But I guess since Aunt Ruthie had died, Mother made an exception and let me stay in the room. But after I jumped up and let every adult in the room know I was listening, I got 'the face' again.

Mother, still sitting in the big chair, looked at me and pointed to the door. This was her way of telling me to go outside on the porch with my other cousins. As I slowly got up and walked out on the porch, the front door creaked like an old field cricket. The adults inside continued to laugh and talk.

I sat on the front porch swing with my big cousin Wendy. She is older than me, but she always let me try on her perfume. I think she is so pretty. All my cousins and brothers were sitting all over the porch and down the porch steps eating cake and laughing about Aunt Ruthie.

Wendy said, "Do you remember how loud she used to laugh?"

Larry jumped up to demonstrate Aunt Ruthie's laugh. He laughed like an old bucking donkey, loud and jerky. We all exploded in laughter. She was so much fun before she got sick. Sonnyboy listened to all our stories about his mom, but he didn't crack a smile. He just sat there. As much as he irritates me, I wanted him to do something. I just wasn't used to seeing him like this.

The night had come and we were still sitting on the front porch. After we talked about Aunt Ruthie, we began to play one of the games she taught us. It's called 'NightHawk.' It's really hide and seek but you played it at night. Everybody would start at home base. One person would count down from twenty and yell, "night hawk!"

The person that did the counting had to find everybody like an old night hawk. It was so fun! You see, night time in the country is not like night time in the city. It is pitch black.

My cousin Wendy is an older girl. She usually doesn't play with us. But tonight she counted down as everybody found a place to hide. Sonnyboy never left his spot on the front porch step. He just sat there while we played.

As the night marched on, my uncles and Aunts started to gather up my cousins. Before long, there was nobody on the front porch except my brothers, Sonnyboy and me. When it got real dark, Mr. Gonzales, Mr. Johnson, and Ms. Flora were the last ones to leave . Mr. Johnson and Mr. Gonzales said their good-byes to Mother and all the family as they walked down the front porch steps and headed to their cars. Mother tried to gather us for bedtime but Ms. Flora would not have it. She made Mother sit down at the kitchen table and take a rest.

Then she made all of us come inside and take baths so we could get ready for bed. While we were all coming and going from the bathroom, Ms. Flora sat down with Mother at the kitchen table. Even though they were talking and drinking ice tea, Ms. Flora could see everything. Everytime we tried to play, Ms. Flora would sit at the table and shake her skinny little fingers back and forth and say, "No, No, get ready for bed children." I think she had eyes in the back of her head. Ms. Flora and Mother continued to talk as each one of us cleaned up for bed. The house began to get quieter and quieter.

When they thought we were all sleep, Ms. Flora got up from the table, hugged Mother, and headed for her car. Although Ms. Flora and Mother watched me go get in the bed, I did not go to sleep. I listened for Ms. Flora's car to pull off. I listened for Mother to cut off all the lights. I listened to her walk down the hallway, and then close her bedroom door.

Mother won't let me have a glass of water after eight o'clock. She says, 'you will wet the bed.' So I was waiting for her to go to bed so I sneak from my bed and get a glass of water.

Mother doesn't know it but I have been sneaking water forever and I have not wet the bed once! Well, maybe I wet the bed once, but I cleaned it up. Anyway, when I heard Mother's bedroom door close tight, I tip-toed down to the dark kitchen and found my water glass. I gently turned on the water faucet and filled my little water glass. I left the light off because I knew Mother or Father would catch me if I turned it on. I turned up my glass of stolen water to my mouth and suddenly out of the darkness, I heard, "What are you doing little girl?"

I jumped so hard my water splashed back in my face and all over my bed clothes.

I gave a little nervous laugh and said, "Father, is that you?"

He stood by the door and turned on the kitchen light.

He said firmly, "Yes, now what are you doing?"

I stood there a moment thinking of what to say. I had to tell the truth because I was caught red-handed with my hand on the water glass and water all over my face and bed clothes. So, I belted out, "Well, I was headed to check on Sonnyboy and thought he might be thirsty. I was getting him a glass of water."

Father filled the 6 foot door frame. He tilted his head folded his arms and looked at me. "Now, Sustahgurl is that the truth cause it looked like you were getting some water for yourself to me."

Before I could lie again, Father sighed, "Never mind, just go to bed. Aunt Ruthie's Homegoing service is going to make for a rough day tomorrow and you need your sleep."

As I put my glass back in the dish holder, I said, "Well, maybe if we all don't go to Aunt Ruthie's Homegoing it wouldn't be a rough day."

Father gave a little smile and said, "Well, we all can't do that Sustahgurl. How do you think that would make Mother feel?"

I turned to Father and said, "Why do we have to go? Mother won't mind all she does is cry over Aunt Ruthie's homegoing. I don't think she wants to go either. Plus it scares me when everybody cries."

Father smiled gently and motioned for me to come and sit with him. He took the dish towel from the table and began to wipe my face. He said, "Sustahgurl, Tomorrow we are all going to say good-bye to Aunt Ruthie at the funeral. I know it's hard sweetheart, but you don't have to be scared. Mother, Sonnyboy, even your uncles might cry. But I want you to know that everything is going to be alright."

He put down the dish towel, petted my thick po-nytail, and kissed me on the cheek. Then he said, "Now come on, get in that bed and no more water!"

I turned toward the door and sighed, "Yes sir."

As I headed to my room, I could feel the hot tears rolling down my face. I thought to myself, I don't want Aunt Ruthie to go home with God. I wanted her here with us. I don't like my Mother feeling sad. As my tears continued to trickle down my face, I turned once more toward Father, "I don't like this."

Father smiled again and said, "I know honey. But think about this, Aunt Ruthie isn't sick anymore and she's probably doing all kinds of cool stuff in heaven. Now go to bed," he said gently.

When I got to my room and lay down, I couldn't stop thinking about what Father said. Aunt Ruthie was probably in heaven playing 'Night Hawk' with all the kids in heaven. I bet you she is making them laugh the way she made us laugh. And you know what else, I think God is going to give her a special job. She is going to be looking after all of us. As I drifted off to sleep, I could hear the gentle cries of my Mother. She was already missing her sister.

CHAPTER FOUR

We were all up bright and early Wednesday morning. And even though Father said Wednesday was going to be a rough day. It started off great for me. I could smell the wonderful smell of pancakes, bacon and eggs. Father made breakfast and it was good! Everybody was at the kitchen table except Mother and Sonnyboy.

As the rest of us sat down to pray and eat Father said, "Children, I don't want any fighting, pushing, shoving or none of that today. We all need to be on our best behavior."

All of us answered Father in a variety of 'yes', 'yep,' or 'o.k. daddy.'

Usually when we get ready to go anywhere, the house can be so loud. Enough to wake the dead. Sorry Aunt Ruthie, but it's true. However, after breakfast, we all listened to Father and got dressed. Nobody fussed or fought! We all walked calmly to the van. Father helped Mother to her front seat. Everybody sat in their assigned seat except me. Floyd let me sit next to the window.

So I watched all the stores and cows zoom by as we headed to the church.   The ride to the church was quiet. Nobody said anything, except Father. He kept talking about being good. Sonnyboy and Mother were still so sad. Neither one of them had much to say. I wanted to help them both but I felt so helpless. When we got to the church, Pastor Hunter greeted everyone with a smile and handshake. He has a deeper voice than Mr. Johnson. He made all the family line up outside the church by two's. We walked in the church together as the music played. We sang a lot. People talked a lot, and people cried a lot. I wasn't scared because Father told me that everything was going to be alright.

After the funeral was over, all of the kids got into two really long cars called limousines. They were really cool. I felt like a rock star! We drove out to the cemetery.

As Pastor Hunter prayed the last prayer, some of my uncles and mother cried one more time really hard as we left Aunt Ruthie there.

I could hear the moans and sniffling noses. Sonnyboy was so upset he screamed and yelled. He kept crying and yelling, "I want my mama. I want my mama." I tried to help him but all the adults came and gathered around him. Uncle Jack picked him up again and packed him back to the limousine. As I watched Uncle Jack put Sonnyboy in his seatbelt, I began to cry. I began to think about how much I loved my mother. I didn't want her to die for a very long time.

The sun was hot and beaming down on everyone as they all headed back to their cars. My uncle's wife, Aunt Sylvia, came and stood by me as I continued to watch Uncle Jack help Sonnyboy.

She slipped her hand in my hand, leaned over, and whispered in my ear, "He's going to be ok precious."

I still just stood there and cried for my cousin be-cause I knew he was going to really miss his mother. The cars in the cemetery made a huge line.

44

Everybody hugged someone and headed back to their car. The ride back in the limousine was very silent. However when we got back to the house, all of our KIN FOLK customers had pitched in again and fixed one, big, gigantic meal. It was even bigger meal than the first meal. It was a meal fit for a King and Queen. There were so many people it looked like Thanksgiving in July. We all ate until we were ready to pop like big balloons. It was great seeing all of our friends and family coming together to help us through such a tough time. Night came again and all of the family and friends soon went home. My brothers were obeying Father and getting ready for bed. I started looking for Mother and found her sitting by herself on the front porch swing. I flopped down on the swing and slipped my hand in her hand. I noticed that she was crying.

I guess she was thinking about her sister. I said, "Mother, are you going to be ok ?"

She smiled through her tears and said "Yes, love, Mommy is going to be just fine."

"Then why do you keep crying?" I asked her.

Mother took a deep breath wiped her tears and said, "Do you remember when our dog Princess died and you and all your brothers were so upset?"

"Yes ma'am, I remember. Princess was a great dog. She was our best friend. She used to go everywhere with us. I still miss her so much."

"Well that's kind of how I feel. Only Aunt Ruthie was my best friend and my sister. I am going to miss my sister and best friend just like you all miss Princess. But don't worry Sustahgurl, everything will be fine, now go and get Mother some sweet tea."

I popped up off the swing feeling better not to see her crying anymore. I headed to the kitchen and found Sonnyboy sitting at the table. He wasn't crying just sitting at the kitchen table. He looked so pitiful. I wanted to do something for him because no matter how mad he can makes me, he is still family.

I had already made up in my mind, I was going to do my best to help Sonnyboy have a good visit. Anybody that "knows" me Sustahgirl when I make up my mind, I am going to do it! As I poured Mother some sweet tea I asked him, "I'm getting mother something to drink, would you also like some tea?"

He didn't say anything. He just drummed his fingers on the table.

"It has lemon slices in it" I said.

He still didn't say anything. He just kept drumming his fingers on the table.

"And it's real sweet" I said. I thought I was being real nice.

Finally he stopped drumming his fingers, dropped his head between his shoulders on the table and mumbled, "Just leave me alone."

Before I turned back to take Mother her tea, I began to think, he's just so sad.

I don't think he's going to be messing with anybody. I just hate to see him so crushed.

I wondered, 'will he ever stop hurting?'

CHAPTER FIVE

Work. Work. Work. It seems like that's all we do! Father's favorite saying is John Maxwell's *'Teamwork makes the dream work!'* So then, every day after we finish our studies and chores, we help Father at the restaurant. Mother and Father keep us all very busy. If we do a tip-top job at the restaurant, Father gives us all an allowance and takes us on a special trip every Saturday.

Well, I should say most of us get an allowance because my younger twin brothers, Garry and George hardly ever get an allowance. They can be jerks because they don't like to work. The only time they look like they are working hard is when Father is looking at them.

Father always says, "I got to keep my eye on you two."

The truth is Father does have to keep his eye on both of them. They both are something else! George is the sneaky twin and Garry is the lazy twin.

George usually sneaks off and gets into trouble. He is really fast. He runs faster than all of us. However the problem is, he knows he is fast. So then, he's always running off without doing his chores. Therefore, Mother and Father give him jobs where they can see him. So his jobs always change. He does whatever job Mother and Father gives him that day. Garry, on the other hand, is lazy and messy! He is so messy, ugh! His clothes always look a mess even though they are clean. He rarely brushes his hair. Floyd teases him all the time and says, "boy you got, bee-bee shots and crycry knots."

Every time Floyd says it, Garry gets as mad as a Florida alligator. It makes everybody laugh because he still will not brush his hair.

My oldest brother, Floyd, takes out the trash. He's pretty strong. He just teases everybody so much. However, he always watches out for us.

My next oldest brother is Jim. I get along with him the best. People say Jim is a little on the chubby side. Mother says Jim is just big boned, but I say he's just fat. Jim's job at home is to clear the kitchen table. However, at the restaurant, he cleans off all the round tables, covers them with table cloths, and puts little baskets of sweet bread on each table. Jim is a good listener, so I think Father likes that and gave him two jobs. He also cleans the high counter. Now the high counter is very important. It is where Mr. Jackson, Mr. Gonzales and all the real smart customers sit and talk about the Bible, politics, the world, and stuff like that. Sometimes, I like to help Jim because I know we are going to sneak and eat some of the sweet bread.

David is younger than me, Floyd and Jim. He's as mean as a snake. We call him the mean moneyman. So then, nobody messes with David! He saves his allowance that Father gives us. Father says that he is going to be rich one day. The rest of us spend it as quick as we get it.

David is the cleanest, meanest, money-having brother I have. We all love him but we don't mess with him too much.

Now Larry is the entertainer of the family. He is always dancing around somewhere.   He loves to make up songs. Whenever anything happens, Larry has a song about it and he never fails to share his songs. Even if we don't want to hear them. One time he made us all listen to a song he wrote about going back to school. It was the silliest little song that only had one line, 'I LOVE SCHOOL, YES I DO.' Still, he was so proud of himself that he lined up all my brothers and me, like we were in church. He made us listen to him sing and demanded a round of applause after he finished.   Larry is younger than Floyd, and taller. He looks like a tall tree with an afro. So since Larry likes being in front of people, Father made him the official greeter of KIN FOLK restaurant. When anyone comes into KIN FOLK, my singing brother Larry greets them. Even though his songs can be a bit annoying, in my opinion, he is a good greeter.

Walter is our baby brother, and he loves to cook. Since he is not old enough to use the stove, Mother and Father allow him to help wash the vegetables and fruits in the kitchen with our cook, Uncle Jack. He is my mother's brother. He loves to cook, just like Mother. They both do all the cooking at KIN FOLK. Uncle Jack teaches Walter a lot of things about how to be a great cook. Uncle Jack and Aunt Ella have almost as many children as Mother and Father but they have seven girls!

Peewee doesn't do much, except stay around Mother. She loves her little dirty doll that she kisses, licks and carries everywhere. The dolls name is Woobie.

Now, my main job is to roll the flatware. You know the forks, spoons and a knife rolled into a napkin. It may not sound like much, but it must be done right. If not right, Father will make me roll them again and I don't like to roll them twice. Actually, I don't really like this job at all. Father always seems to give me the same job.

What I really want to do is be 'the checker.' The checker gets to go around and check to make sure everybody is doing their job. Father usually lets David or Floyd do it, but I know I could do it! However, Father feels I'm too young for the job. Today, Father asked me to get all my brothers together for a family meeting at the restaurant. We never have a family meeting unless something is going to happen, major!

Our house is pretty big. I mean, it is eleven of us, well now twelve. So I started first in the place where I would find most all of them, the family room. Our family room is like the place where everybody can do anything. We play games, watch TV, and work on the computer, just about everything happens in the family room. I poked my head in the room. Floyd had George on the stool, cutting his hair.

Larry was singing some song he made up, and Garry was hiding under the couch from Floyd. He never wants his hair cut.

"Father said we are going to have a family meeting at the restaurant." I said.

Floyd continued to cut Georges hair and said, "What's wrong?"

I shrugged my shoulders and said, "I don't know he just told me to round up everybody. That means you too, Garry. I see you under that couch."

As Larry continued to sing his song, Garry peeped out from under the coach and said, "I'm not coming out cause Floyd is gonna cut my hair."

I snickered at Garry as he pulled back under the couch. He looked like a tortoise poking his head out of its shell. Floyd gives all my brothers a haircut. However, Garry is the only one that hides when it's his turn for a haircut.

Floyd said, "You ought to want to get that hair cut! It's wooly as a sheep's butt!

Garry yelled from under the couch, "No it's not! Mother says it's just thick!"

As I headed for the Kitchen, I could still hear Floyd fussing at Garry.

When I got to the kitchen, I flung myself in the room and saw Jim making a sandwich. Walter was on the step stool washing his apple over the sink.

I said, "Father said come to the restaurant for a family meeting. As Jim prepared to take a big bite out of his sandwich he said, "Do you know what he wants?"

"Not really?" I said.

As Jim munched on his sandwich he said, "you know something, so spill it!"

I turned around and looked behind me to see if anyone was listening and whispered, "I think Father is going to let me be the checker at the restaurant this time. I been begging for that job. It's much better than rolling the flatware, and I really want it. He's going to announce it to every-body!" I smiled and swung my arms in the air like a dramatic gymnast.

Walter stepped off the stool with his freshly clean apple and said, "Sustahgurl do you think Daddy is going to give me a better job too?"

I put my hands on my hips, smiled and said to my little brother, "Whatever job Father gives you it's a big job!" He gave me a front toothless smile as he took a bite into his big red apple.

Jim was sitting at the kitchen table. He leaned back in his chair and laughed, "Sustahgurl you gonna get that same job that you always get, the flatware. Anyway, why would Father call a family meeting just to give you a job he already told you that you are too young for?"

I stomped my foot and glared at Jim and snorted, "I am not too young. I can do this job. You will see. He is going to give me that job and announce it to everybody." I flung my arms wide open and bowed my head.

Jim just laughed again and said, "Ok Sustahgurl, whatever you say."

I stomped off and yelled as I headed to the basement, "Quit laughing at me and I can do that job no matter what you or anybody else thinks!"

Still mad about Jim laughing at me, I headed to the basement. When I got to the bottom of the steps, I saw Sonnyboy with his feet on Mother's table, clipping his toe nails. David was stuffing clothes in the washer. It was his day to wash his clothes.

I looked at Sonnyboy and said, "That is disgusting! You are supposed to clip toenails in the bathroom! UGH! You are so gross!"

David still stuffing clothes in the washer said, "Sustahgurl, what do you want?"

Still angry, I remembered what I was supposed to say and spouted, "Father is calling a family meeting. He wants everybody at the restaurant including both you knuckleheads!"

Sonnyboy continued to clip his toenails as David finished putting his clothes in the washer "Dang what's wrong with you? You come down here with an at-ti-tude! Ain't nobody did nothing to you little girl."

I puffed my hair out of my face and snapped back, "I am not a little girl! Anyway all of ya'll getting on my nerves."

David grunted back, "I didn't do anything to you."

I just looked at him and said, "Both of ya'll need to be there, knuckleheads!"

David turned and pointed his finger at me and said, "Keep on, I ain't gonna be too many more knuckleheads. I going to tell Mother that you down here name calling."

I rolled my eyes at David and stomped back up the steps and out the front door. Since KIN FOLK sits directly beside our big house, I decided to walk over to the restaurant by myself. Anybody that sits at our high counter can see the whole world of Limestone County.

KINFOLK

RESTUARANT

As I walked up to the KIN FOLK restaurant, I noticed Father sitting at the high counter through the window. He was working on some paper work I also noticed there were not any cars in front of the building.

When I got inside Father said, "Hey Love, how is my baby girl?"

Since the restaurant is so close to the house, it didn't take the rest of them too long to get to the meeting. So then, before I could tell Father what was wrong, all my noisy brothers flooded the room.

Our restaurant is filled with round tables with neatly pressed white table cloths on each table. Father stopped his paperwork and told us to sit down. He moved to the middle of the room like he was going to make a speech. He was smiling ear to ear. I wasn't as mad anymore because I just knew Father was going to make me 'the checker' for the restaurant!

The room began to buzz with all our voices. We all were squirming in our chairs as we talked to one another. Garry and George were running up and down the aisles touching each table.

Father stopped smiling and yelled, "Hey everybody! Quiet down! George and Garry sit down right now! I have a big announcement."

His face was twisted up because we were being so loud. The room got really quiet and everybody was focused on Father. A family meeting is always something big. The last family meeting we had was when Mother and Father told us Peewee was coming. I hope they are not having another baby. I love all my family but I don't need another sister.

Father broke the silence and said, "Well it's official! KIN FOLK is going to be closed for a couple of weeks!" Everybody yelled, "Alright! Cool! and Yes!"

Father waived his hands for us to quiet down again.

He said, "I want to give the family time to heal. However, I also wanted to let you know Sonnyboy is a part of this family. I do not want anybody giving him a hard time."

Father paused and looked at me like I'm going to be the one causing a problem. Then He said, "Also I am going to let Sonnyboy be the checker."

My mouth dropped and I blurted out, "Are you serious! That's my job!"

Jim snickered. Sonnyboy gave a tiny grin. I just sat there, gave them both an evil glare and pushed back in my chair with my arms folded tight. I squished my face so tight because I felt this was not right!

CHAPTER SIX

What is the world coming to? I mean really! Our restaurant is closed and when it does open back up, Sonnyboy gets to be the checker. He may think he's going to boss me around but I have news for him! I am not having it! Even though I was mad about Father's choice, it has been really quiet around the restaurant and the house. Our family and friends are not over to our house every single day. So then, all the big meals are over until the restaurant re-opens. Mother seems to be getting a little better. Everything is getting back to normal except, Sonnyboy. He still seems to be in a daze. He knew I wanted the checker job. Any other time if he figured out he got something I wanted, he would tease me until I screamed! However, he didn't mess with me not even once! I know I complain all the time about his annoying ways but, I would at least like for him to show signs of life. He just sits around doing nothing. No smart remarks.

No chilling grin. No plunks, pokes, or pushes. He is, well I'm almost afraid to say it, boring! Since the restaurant is closed, everybody has a little more free time to do whatever. Father has already started to focus on the big grand re-opening of the restaurant. See, Father is more of the business manager of KIN FOLK, and he doesn't cook too much or too good. So since Mother and Uncle Jack have been taking it easy, we have not been eating like we usually eat. Nobody complains except Jim. I think the restaurant being closed has him upset the most.

"I'm dying." Jim moaned, "I'm dying for food." He held his belly and rolled over in the grass.

"Jim, you are not dying. Plus, we already ate."

Jim turned and looked at me with squinty eyes and said, "Sustagirl, red beans and rice is hardly a meal. And plus, Father thinks red beans and rice goes with everything. Eggs, bologna, even cake. I can't take it! I want my meatloaf, cornbread, cabbage, greens, chess pies, sweet potatoes, mashed potatoes. OH I'm so hungry. I need to eat! I'm dying for real food over here."

Jim rolled back over on to his back under the big tree in the front yard and blankly stared at the sky. I laid beside him smacking stickers in my sticker book.

I said, "Why don't you just quit that complaining right now. You know you are not dying. If you didn't eat up everything in sight you probably wouldn't feel so hungry. Plus, if anybody is dying it's me! I can't believe Father gave Sonnyboy my checker job. Do you know how he is going to torture me when we re-open! Ugh!"

Jim rolled over and moaned again and said, "I am so hungry."

I turned away from my sticker book, looked up and said, "Jim are you even listening to me?"

"I can't be listening to you and dying of starvation at the same time!" Jim said.

"Well if it makes you feel better, I also overheard Father say he is going to be re-opening the restaurant soon. So you don't have too much longer to starve," I said.

Jim sat straight up with a huge goofy smile. The excitement made his eyebrows rise high on his forehead. He smiled and said, "Are you for real Sustahgirl! Did he really say that?"

I rolled my eyes while turning to Jim to say, "Naw for fake! Yes for real and when KIN FOLK re-opens my life is over because Sonnyboy will be the checker!" I threw myself down on the sticker book and moaned like I was in pain.

Jim smiled, threw up the victory arms and shouted, " Thank You Jesus! NO MORE RED BEANS AND RICE!" He jumped up on his feet and poked his head out, back and forth and to the left and right. He tucked his hands under his armpits and walked around singing, "We gonna EAT. We gonna EAT." He looked just like the peacocks that strut around in the zoo. I giggled at him for one second and then I huffed and puffed my face like a blow fish. I reached up and scratched my head so hard that my hair wiggled loose from my ponytails. I said, "Did you hear one thing I said?"

Jim stopped his victory dance and looked down on me and warned, "Sustahgurl, don't go there."

I looked up from my sticker book as said, "Go where?"

"Everytime you get mad and stuff you get all puffed face like a fish. Then you start scratching your head getting your hair all messed up. Sonnyboy is still hurting for his mother. He don't care about you or your precious little checker job. All he has been doing is sitting around and moping. I'm surprised you didn't notice! Yesterday when everybody was playing he just sat on the porch. He wasn't even smiling. I wish I knew what to say to him" Jim said, as he laid back down in the grass and rolled back over on his belly.

I laid my sticker book to the side of me and laid back down next to Jim under the big tree and said, "Well, yeah I guess you are right. He usually laughs at everything that gets on my nerves. But when he found out I wanted that checker job, he didn't laugh once."

Maybe He doesn't want to prank no more. I mean his mom did die. Maybe he's all pranked out. What do you think?" Jim shrugged his shoulders to my question as we sat on the ground under the big tree. When all of a sudden, we heard the most humungous yell! We both jumped up from the front yard grass and started running toward the sound. We quickly were joined by the rest of the family running from all parts of the front and backyard. As I ran, my thoughts were running all over the place, was someone sick? I kept hearing the yells. Was someone hurt? The yelling got louder as we got to the back side of the house.

We found Uncle Jack covered in water and fighting to turn off a pulsating water hose gone wild. The hose seemed to be going crazy. It was flipping all over the ground. Every time Uncle Jack tried to reach for the water hose, it would soak him even more and move to another spot. He was yelling and carrying on.

We laughed as he yelled and fussed at the water hose like it was a naughty child. The harder he tried to turn the water hose off the wetter he became. Uncle Jack began yelling louder and slipping around in the gushing water stream. By this time, the whole family was in the backyard watching and trying to find out what the ruckus was all about.

Father said, "Jack what you are doing?"

Uncle Jack continued to wrestle with the water hose which by this time seemed to look like it had a mind of its own.

Uncle Jack still soaked and wrestling with the hose yelled, "I can't get the dumb thing to turn off!"

Father walked over to the water hose and simply turned the hose off. Mother was laughing so hard at Uncle Jack she could hardly stand up.

"Lena, it is not funny." Uncle Jack said firmly. Father covered his mouth but you could see that he was laughing at Uncle Jack as well.

All of a sudden everybody broke out in a knee pounding laughter. We all pointed at Uncle Jack and his super mad face. As everyone began to laugh even louder and harder, Uncle Jack wiped his face and finally cracked a smile that turned into laughter as well.

Father snorted, "Jack what were you trying to do?"

Uncle Jack still laughing said, "I was trying to clean these dang gone garbage cans. I turned on the water hose and it went crazy. Every time I got closer to it seemed like it would jump to someplace else. I tried to turn the sprayer off but was like it was jammed or something."

As everyone's laughter died down, I asked myself the question, 'could this be it? Was this him? Did Sonnyboy strike his first prank and everybody missed it?'

This would have qualified for Sonnyboy as a prank. I was sure of it. At that moment, I felt that the pranks had begun! I glared around the yard counting all my brothers. They were all still laughing at Uncle Jack. Mother was still cracking up about Uncle Jack's soaked clothes. I even saw Father laughing and trying to help Uncle Jack dry off. But the one person I did not see was Sonny-boy! This was a classic Clarence, 'Sonnyboy' prank! It had his name all over it. Why did my family not see that this was the start of a series of poisonous pranks that would take over the world? OK. Well maybe not that serious. But everybody was so distracted by the laughter they didn't even notice that the little demon child was nowhere to be found. But I knew it was him. I knew that somewhere under a bush, behind a door or in that huge backyard was an aggravating boy that was laughing at us all. As the family continued to settle down from the silly moment, I closed my eyes. I shook my head as my ponytails wagged back and forth because I knew that this was a sad day.

It would only get worse before it got better. The
pranks had started! Did my family even know
what had happen? The terror had begun!

CHAPTER SEVEN

It was three weeks! Three! Three weeks, two days, and 37 minutes of pranks, jokes, water balloons, Ugh! Lord knows I wanted him to feel better, but I hate him! No, that's not true, I don't hate my cousin. He is family and I really do love him but, he's still the most annoying person! It was just as I suspected, prank after annoying prank! I started to hate Sonnyboy! Ugh! No that's not true. I HATE his ways. I know I said I made up in my mind to help him have a good visit, but he's impossible! He pulls my ponytails and runs. If I have candy, he begs for it. He is always convincing my twin brothers, George and Garry to pull his dumb finger and he lets out these yucky farts that hover in the room like a ten foot green monster. Pee-yew!

He plunks my little sister Peewee, until she sounds off screams like a bottle rockets on the fourth of July.

Jim found out it was Sonnyboy that pranked Uncle Jack with the water hose. He even pranked Uncle Jack again! Only this time he used stagnant water balloons over the restaurant's kitchen door. It was a stinky mess. He got a spanking for that one. My entire soul was happy that day. All of my brothers except Jim and David have adopted Sonnyboy as their newest buddy and ring leader. They call him funny Sonny, but I call him the 'The Annoying Sonnyboy' which should make him mad, but he loves it!

The most annoying and obnoxious Sonnyboy trait is his big, stupid, fat, cat grin. He always has this enormous grin that really bugs me! I thought Aunt Ruthie's death changed him because he was so boring. He wasn't even grinning but he hasn't changed. His mama is dead and he's still back to his aggravating, annoying, obnoxious, bothersome, irritating, worrisome ways. Today Sonnyboy has been picking on me the whole day. Oh Lord, help me!

I had to get away so I went outside on the porch steps. All my brothers know my 'mad spot.' They all just leave me alone when they see me pouting on the steps. But today I am joined by David, he's the mean brother. Well maybe not mean but he doesn't play much. He's more of the serious type. He saw me in my 'mad spot' and walked over and said, "What's wrong with you?"

"Nothing" I snorted.

David put one foot on the porch and said, "Well something's going on with you sitting here in your 'I'm mad' seat with your puff fish face. So what's wrong?"

I folded my arms tightly, looked up and said, "Really, did you just call me a fish face? Whatever! Never mind! It's just too many people in this house."

David smiled, sat down and said, "Oh you mean Sonnyboy."

I unfolded my arms and threw them both up in the air and said, "Today he just would not leave me alone. For two hours, he has repeated everything I said. Every time me, George and Garry would say something he would repeat it. So annoying! David, ordinarily one more person in our house would not normally make a difference, but Sonnyboy is not normal! Everybody just wants to make him feel better. Nobody pays attention to the stuff he does and nobody even knows I'm alive! Even though he was repeating what the twins said, they thought it was the funniest thing ever. I told them don't laugh, and they usually listen to me. But when Sonnyboy is around, Oh NOOOO they only listen to him. They kept on laughing at his stupid pranks! It makes me mad!"

I stomped my foot and folded my arms like a genie.

David stood up on the porch and said, "Sustahgurl, you're jealous he is getting some attention. You don't have to be jealous. We all love you. You are our Sustahgurl. But we also love Sonnyboy. You need to quit letting him bother you so much."

"I am not jealous of him! But David, he does have everybody, including Mother, thinking he is this perfect angel. I do agree with Mother and everybody, he is perfect, a perfect pest! A perfect nuisance, basically a perfect..... Pain!" I pouted again and stomped my foot on the porch.

"Sustahgurl, you're tripping. He just lost his mom. We are just trying to make him feel at home. Have some heart."

"See, you are thinking just like Mother and the rest of them! Mother feels sorry for him because Aunt Ruthie died. You feel sorry for him. All ya'll feel sorry for him. Well I don't feel sorry for him. I still say he is annoying!"

David grinned again and patted me on the head like a little sick puppy as he walked across the porch into the house. He turned to me and said through the screen door, "Don't be so serious and try to have fun with Sonnyboy. He's not that bad."

I looked at the closed door and thought to myself, 'Is he serious?'

After David went in the house, I got up from my mad spot to go look for Mother. I was going to tell her how I really felt about this Sonnyboy thing. Little did I know I was about to go through the worse Sonnyboy prank ever!

It all started when I found Mother getting ready to fix lunch.   Sonnyboy and my other brothers were outside playing football. Since I was not invited, I helped Mother make angel snacks for lunch!

Angel snacks are really fried bologna sandwiches with Swiss cheese. Mother has made them for us since we were really little.

They are very easy to make. First you cut two diagonal slits on the top sides to make the head that form a wide 'V.' Then you cut two slits on the sides at the bottom. This makes the gown and the arms with wings!

Mother said the real reason you cut the bologna this way is to keep your meat from bubbling up when you fry it. But, we like to call them angel snacks because the bologna looks like an angel after you cut it. We even cut the bread so it looks like a white gown. This is a snack she usually makes but today since I was not playing football, she let me help her. Mother listened to me rant and rave all about, Sonnyboy! She just continued to help me as we made lunch. Even though I was upset about Sonnyboy, I like to cook like my Mother. I was so excited about helping her make lunch.

My brothers love these sandwiches until, THE ANNOYING SONNYBOY!

After we finished making lunch, Mother said, "Sustahgurl, go call Sonnyboy and your brothers for lunch while I go to the basement and put some clothes in the washer."

So I went out the creaky front porch door and screamed to the top of my lungs, "TIME TO EAT!"

My twin brothers George and Garry screamed back, " WHAT ARE WE EATING?"

I said with Christmas excitement in my voice "Angel snacks and chips!"

This is the first snack I have made that my brothers really like! They came running up the front porch stairs. Except Sonnyboy, he slowly climbed up the steps. He walked in the front door with one shoe off because he is always plays the kicker when they play football.

 I saw that my brothers were headed straight for the table so I quickly shouted, "Nope, go wash your hands!"

Everybody pushed and squeezed in the guest bathroom washing their hands. They all came back to the kitchen table and sat down when Sonnyboy yelled, "Why do you all like these nasty sandwiches?"

All my brothers began to answer Sonnyboy's question like they didn't really like the sandwiches. Even though two minutes ago, they were racing to the kitchen table like track stars. I am not gonna lie, that made me mad! Anyway, after making fun of my sandwiches and giggling about how they looked like angels, my brother Larry, who loves to make up songs, made up a little song. The song started off sounding like a church choir singing in perfect harmony to the French tune Fara Shaka. All my other brothers chimed in, "THEY ARE NASTY, THEY ARE NASTY, YES THEY ARE. YES THEY ARE…. VERY VERY NASTY. VERY VERY NASTY. YES THEY ARE. YES THEY ARE. "

They were all making me mad. My face puffed up and I blurted out loudly and firmly," THEY ARE NOT NASTY!"

Sonnyboy laughed with all his teeth showing and jeered, "Yes they are!"

Sonnyboy and I went back and forth yelling like two boxers. "Yes, they are!" Sonnyboy shouted.

"No they are not!" I screamed. Finally, Sonnyboy belted out a comment like a drill sergeant in the Army, "those sandwiches are so nasty they probably taste worse than my foot."

Then it happened! I don't know why he did it, but Sonnyboy did it. It was mean! He made me so mad I could have lit fire crackers from my mouth!

I turned to my brothers and screamed, with my fists clinched, and my face squished, "IT DOES NOT TASTE LKE A FOOT."

Sonnyboy smiled again with all of his gazillion teeth showing and hollered, "Yes it does, SEEEEEE! Taste it!"

He took his big, nasty, scaly, stinky, sweaty, gross, recently finished football playing foot and put it on my sandwich! All my brothers broke out in laughter.

I jumped up like a Chinese Ninja girl ready for battle! Mother was still in the basement doing laundry, so she couldn't hear all the commotion because of the washer and the dryer making noises. The moment seemed to move in slow motion. My brothers were still laughing so hard they were holding each other up. George and Garry were laughing and rolling on their backs in the floor like rolly polly bugs. There are many things that do not bother me. I am not bothered by mice, snakes, bugs, bats, or rats, but I hate, and I do mean hate, to be laughed at. I stood there and glared at Sonnyboy in full Ninja fighting stance. I took the entire bowl of potato chips and declared war on Sonnyboy.

Potato chips flew all over the room as I dashed for Sonnyboy. His mouth dropped as he ran out of the kitchen and down the hallway. My brothers continued to laugh as they ran after me and sonnyboy . I was hot on his trail as I chased him right to the front door. Sonnyboy burst out the front porch door like a thief running from the police.

George, the fastest twin, was leading my pack of brothers through the smashed chips as they chased after me.

Sonnyboy made me so mad that I chased him all the way to the lake. When we all arrived at the lake, all my brothers and Sonnyboy were out of breathe but they were still laughing and pointing at me and Sonnyboy.

Sonnyboy was from the city. And I think all that country air started making him cough, choke, pant, spit, and speak in a choppy voice, "OK ...Sustahgurl ...that's enough, we.. Can't ..Go.. Any further... It's over. I was just messing with you."

"NO it's not over!" I said as I snapped my two long ponytails back with my hand on my hip, you put your big foot in my food!"

As he still tried to laugh through the coughing and panting, "Dang Sustahgurl, it was just a joke, I'm sorry."

Now I knew better than that. Sonnyboy was not sorry. He was just sorry he was caught and trapped! And I was determined I was going to teach him a lesson.

While my brothers continued to laugh and giggle, I looked at Sonnyboy and yelled, "You are not sorry, but I AM going to make you sorry."

By this time, mother had come up from the basement and saw the mess we left in the kitchen. She ran with Peewee all the way to the lake. When she reached us, she was mad as a wet hornet and out of breathe. Her face was shiny and sweaty. As she bent over putting Peewee down, she put her hand on her knees and spoke slow, angrily, and paused long enough to belt out, " You...all...better..quit...picking... at... each...other.... so...much....let's get back..to the..house...and ...all.. of... you...are...going...to ... clean...up my...kitchen!"

So, I slowly turned around eyeballing all my brothers and Sonnyboy. I was careful not to say anything because I didn't want to make Mother any madder than she already was. I just stared at them all with a mean mug and didn't say a word.

As we all headed back to the house, I could still hear my brothers trying to hold back their laughs at me. Sonnyboy was snickering, and I was boiling like hot water on a gas stove.

Every step closer to the house made me boil the more. I thought to myself, 'who does he think he is? Everybody is laughing at me and, he ruined my angel snacks! I don't know how I am going to do it, but I am going to get him back!'

As we came close to the house, I spied a little surprise that put a tiny grin on my face. At that moment, a plan popped in my head to get back at that annoying Sonnyboy.

CHAPTER EIGHT

When we got back to the house, I made sure my little surprise was safe. The rest of the day was spent cleaning the crushed potato chips, and angel snacks that were all over the floor. Sonnyboy really thought that he got the best of me and the entire event was over. I however had other plans because I knew that my cousin was from the city and he did not like furry, fuzzy, slimy, scaly, or slithery things. I had a devious plan to get him back for making everybody laugh at me.

All the boys share one big room. Father built six sets of bunk beds that line both sides the walls. So even though I only have seven brothers, we always have extra beds for guests.

Mother makes us clean up every night! We wash clothes, clean the kitchen after dinner, take baths, spruce of the bathroom after taking baths, and prepare for bed and the next day. That night while everyone was completing this nightly ritual, I sneaked off kitchen duty to my room to get my little surprise for Sonnyboy and put it in his bed.

I was giggling so hard to myself I could hardly keep quiet.

Peewee and I share a room next to Mother and Father's room on the first floor, but she was in the bed with Mother and Father. All my brothers and Sonnyboy had already finished their chores and taken their baths. They were upstairs about to get in bed, so nobody saw me sneak back up the steps. I wasn't going to miss this! I peeked from behind the door as I watched all my brothers one by one get into bed. Sonnyboy was the last one to take a bath. He always does these strange stretches before he goes to bed. He came in to the bedroom and stretched his head and neck like a little goose. He continued to stretch his arms and legs until he sat down on the bed.

Sonnyboy puffed his pillow two or three times and stretched his arms one final time before he lay down. His head hit the pillow first. Then he put his feet under the covers. He proceeded to scoot down in the bed and did a slight wiggle in the bed to get under the covers just right.

He made a slight giggled sound and made a quick turn in the bed. He sat straight up and I could see the white of his eyes pop from behind the door AND THEN IT HAPPENED!   He let out a scream that shook the house. He jumped up and out of that bed and began this weird smacking, swatting, jumping, skipping dance while he screamed to the top of his lungs like a little school girl. He wouldn't quit.

He kept yelling and screaming, smacking, swatting, and jumping all around his bed.

My brothers began to pop up in their beds one by one. They all awoke to Sonnyboy doing this weird skipping, smacking, jumping dance.

A huge roar of laughter broke out in room. I fell behind the door rolling around in the floor laughing at Sonnyboy.

Mother and Father came running past me in to the room. They both had frowns on their faces.

Father said with a loud voice and scrunched face, "What's going on?"

My brothers all began to speak at once. Sonny-boy was still doing this skipping, smacking, swatting, jumping dance while he screamed to the top of his lungs like a young school girl. He kept pointing to the bed and making goofy words that didn't make sense. Father leaned over and turned the covers back and there was my little surprise. A little green garter snake slithered around at the foot of Sonnyboy's bed. I felt like saying, "GOTCHA".

Father yelled, "Now, who put a snake in this boy's bed?"

My brothers' roars of laughter came down to a whisper. They all looked at one another but said nothing. You could hear a pin drop in that room.

As I was trying to sneak back down the steps, Mother caught a glimpse of me and demanded me to come to her, "Mary Ethel Green! Come here right now!"

I could hear in her voice that she had moved past 'the face' and was in 'I'm going to get you' mode.

As I inched my way to her, all I could think about was, 'he started it and I finished it. I don't want to get into trouble.'

Again, I won't go so far as to say I am a perfectly good girl. I have naughty ways sometimes. I sometimes do things that get me into trouble. I don't start out trying to find trouble. It finds me. Father and mother spend a lot of time reminding me of these troublesome things that I should not do.

I made my way to mother with one thought on my mind, 'he started it!'

By the time I was in front of Mother, who has a way of making me feel like a teeny tiny baby, she huffed, "did you have anything to do with this?"

My mind began to race like a race car for answers. In my mind, I began to talk fast to myself. 'Should I tell her the truth that Sonnyboy really ANNOYS ME!

Should I tell her how he put his nasty foot on my angel snack? Or should I tell her I was playing outside and found the snake. Maybe, the snake got loose, in the house, and it crawled from downstairs to upstairs. It slithered into Sonnyboy's bed. Naw, she's gonna know that's a lie. Or maybe I should just say, 'NO.'

The problem with all these answers were they were LIES. But even though I knew that I should tell the truth the LIE flew out my mouth like a little white bird escaping its cage. I tucked my head and made circles with my feet and said, "no mother, I didn't have anything to do with it."

When my mother is really mad, she pinches her lips real close together and her nostrils open really round like perfect little circles. She stood in her robe with her hands on her hips, as Peewee, who had made her way upstairs with her woobie, hugged Mother's leg.

"Sustahgurl! Now, is that the truth?" She pressed me harder.

Lies are like hamburger sandwiches, you just keep stacking stuff on it. Why didn't I just tell the truth? Why didn't I take the chance and tell Mother what really happened? All I could think about was how Sonnyboy had all my brothers laughing at me and I just couldn't let him get away with that. So, I looked Mother straight in the face and guess what I did? I lied AGAIN.

"Yes ma'am that's the truth." I whispered and tucked my head again and made circles with my feet.

 By this time, Father was trying to help Sonnyboy calm down. My brothers were quiet but still snickering at Sonnyboy. Jim knew I did it. I think the rest of my brothers knew I did it too. And I am almost certain Mother knew I did it. She stood straight like the crossing guard at school. She pointed for me to go to my room. Her arm seemed to move in slow motion. She gave me 'the face' as I passed! She didn't question me about the lie. She didn't even ask me one final time for the truth. She just didn't say anything to me.

I hate when she does that. As I passed her by she was scaring me like the doctors at the hospital in all the white coats. She didn't say anything but her face was saying, 'I am going to get you good!'

CHAPTER NINE

There are three things that will happen in the Green household. Number one, everybody goes to school and work. Number two, everybody does their chores. The third and most important is number three, everybody and I do mean every-body, goes to church! I don't mind. I like going to church. So much happened on Saturday I just wanted to think about something else. I still felt bad about the lie I told Mother. I felt good that I made Sonnyboy cry. To be honest, I still felt like he asked for it!

It was Sunday morning and things seemed to have calmed down a little in the house. Mother called us all to the breakfast table and she kept looking at me. It was like she knew something or she could see LIAR wrote in big fat red crayon on my forehead. She sat down at the kitchen table with her cup of coffee and sipped it ever so slow. She peeped over her coffee cup and said, "Is there anything you want to tell me, Sustahgurl?"

Now I knew Mother knew something, but I was not volunteering any information. My face and stomach dropped and good heavens I lied again, "No ma'am," I said.

Mother sipped her coffee again and pinched her lips with those same perfect little circle nostrils, and snapped, "O.K., go get in the van."

As we loaded up the van, everybody was quiet except Jim. He and Floyd were still my van buddies. Once we were on the van Jim leaned over and whispered, "Why did you lie? You should've just told the truth. You know she gonna catch you!"

I whispered back to Jim, "Just be quiet, I don't want to talk about it. Plus I still say he should have quit messing with me! He started it."

"Even if he did start it, you didn't have to lie!" Jim whispered, "All I'm going to say is, Mother's gonna get you!"

I flopped back in the seat disgusted that they knew. To make matters worse, Floyd leaned over from the other side and said, "Mother is gonna get you good little lie girl." He giggled like an evil clown.

As we headed to Church, I watched Sonnyboy look out the window. He seemed really mad. My other brothers didn't have much to say. I was scared one or all of them were going to tell mother or father that I put that snake in Sonnyboy's bed.

When we pulled on the Church lot and parked the van, I jumped off the van and ran across the big parking lot to Church School. I was so afraid Sonnyboy or one of my brothers was going to rat me out.

Mother stopped to talk to Ms. Crystal. Before I went into the building, I looked back and wondered what mother was saying to Ms. Crystal. I wanted to run back across the lot , waving my hands wildly and screaming, 'I did it! I did it!'

! I put the snake in Sonnyboy's bed. Instead, I just sighed slowly like a leaking bicycle tire and sulked all the way to my church school class. My head was tucked low and my shoulders shrugged even lower because I was officially a liar.

After Miss Crystal finished talking to Mother, she bounced into the room with a big smile and books held tightly to her chest. Miss Crystal's was so sweet. She was just like our Sunday school room, bright and colorful. She looked around the room and said, "Children we have a special project today." She walked across the room in her multi-colored dress, sneakers and said, "I need everybody to make a circle on the floor."

Miss Crystal makes all of our lessons fun. One time we went to the local ice cream parlor for a treat. We do all sorts of things like read stories, play games, talk, stuff like that.

All of our lessons help us to learn about the Bible and how to do better. So, church school is like regular school, but you learn about the Bible and stuff.

The entire class quickly made a circle in the floor. Miss Crystal's class was the biggest class at the church. She had walls filled with the pictures we had drawn. She put all the books of the Bible on the wall in that plastic stuff so nobody could tear them up. She also had a food pantry. She had all kinds of treats. After she collected all her food supplies for the day, she came back to the circle. She sat in her teachers chair with paper towels, a stack of fruit roll-ups and white cards. All the children in the circle were laughing, and talking when Miss Crystal said, " I need two quiet volunteers."

The room became quite as a mouse as every-one's hand flew up in the air, including my hand. Miss Crystal spied around the room and with a long pause she said, "O.K., I pick Tommy and Sustahgurl."

I was so excited I felt like one of the contestants on a TV game show because I never get picked for anything. Miss Crystal gave us the paper towels and fruit roll-ups to pass out to every kid in the class.

After each person had their supplies, Tommy and I joined the circle. Miss Crystal said, "now open your fruit roll-up and place it on your paper towel but do not eat the candy."

We all moaned and groaned because we wanted to eat the rollup.

She said, "O.K. class today we are going to play a game call 'TRUTH OR LIE.' I am going to read from my stack of cards and I want you to tell me if what I've read is a "TRUTH OR LIE" Now if it is a lie, we are all going to roll up one tiny piece of our fruit roll-up. Tommy and I were back in the circle participating in the game. It was fun at first as we continued to roll up our fruit roll-up to all the lies. The roll-ups were getting bigger and bigger. The class shouted answers to Miss Crystal's questions.

After several minutes of play Miss Crystal said, "O.K. class I want everybody to look at their fruit roll-up and tell me what you see."

Everybody said something different. Miss Crystal gave us the best answer.

114

She said, "All those answers are very good, but I want you to see how lies keep "rolling up" until you have a bunch of lies. And just like the fruit rollup, you don't know what's the truth and what a lie because it's all bunched up together. The Bible says in Colossians 3:9 'Do not lie to one another, for you have put off the old self with its habits.' Lying is a bad habit. It makes it hard for people to trust you when you lie. God wants us to tell the truth to one another even if it means that we are going to get in trouble. Lying is an old habit that we don't do anymore, so let's start being better by doing what class?" the whole class yelled "Doing Better!"

"And how are we going to do better?" Miss Crystal asked.

The class shouted, "Don't lie tell the truth!"

Miss Crystal looked around the room and smiled then said, "O.K. now you can eat your fruit roll up."

After church, Mother made sure we all got back on the van. We were all headed home because Father needed help with the Sunday crowd. No one said much on the ride back home. All I could think about was how all my lies had rolled up and gotten other people all wrapped up in my lies! I decided I didn't want to lie anymore. I didn't like the way it made me feel. I didn't really know how to fix the lies. I already had told Mother so many lies, and what was she going to do to me when she found out that I lied?

CHAPTER TEN

Our restaurant is back open! We are going to
have a big crowd today. Today's menu at the restaurant is wonderful. Uncle Jack and Mother
fixed sweet potatoes, sweet potato pies, greens,
sweet ham, meatloaf, macaroni and cheese, hot
water cornbread, snap peas, and mashed potatoes. Lord have mercy!

Our restaurant is a beautiful white building that
sits next door to our house . We have plenty of
parking and Father says, 'Everybody likes a Sunday drive!' He must be right because we always
have a crowd on Sunday.   Today is a bigger crowd
than normal. This is the first day we are back
open since Aunt Ruthie died. We feed much of
the community on Sundays but, we always go to
church first. Everybody helps on this day.   Father
says that 'God forgives us for working on Sunday
because we are also helping families by serving
quality dinner for dirt cheap prices.' We charge
for the dinner so we can keep providing dinners,
but the customers get so much good food on
their plate, they don't mind.

While we were waiting for the grand re-open, Jim has been his self. He could hardly wait for the restaurant to open.

"Sustahgurl, help me fix all these tables. I'm ready to eat!" barked Jim.

"Jim, do you ever think about anything but food?" I asked.

"As a matter of fact" Jim said, "just today, I was thinking about that whopper of lie you told to Mother the other day."

"I know Jim. I feel bad enough about it. You are just making it worse." I said.

Jim said, "You know you need to go over there and talk to him. He could have gotten you into a whole lot of trouble but he didn't. And don't you want to know why?"

Jim had a good point. I really wasn't sure why Sonnybody didn't tell on me. He certainly had the upper hand. I knew he loved having the upper hand on anyone.

I left Jim setting up all of the round tables and table cloths. I walked up to Sonnyboy and started helping him with the flatware. This was my job, but somehow Mother put us both on the same job. As we stood rolling the flatware, we said nothing and worked in silence. We stood several minutes just rolling the flatware in napkins. He was pushing my buttons just by the way he rolled the flatware. It was wrong. Plus, I wanted to talk to him but I didn't know how to start the conversation. So I just said anything.

"You are not rolling them right." I snapped "you are supposed to put them on the end of the napkin and then roll on the diagonal."

"So what! Does it really matter?" Sonnyboy snapped back after he dumped two forks in the napkin.

"Yes it does! Mother will make us do them again! Plus I got other stuff I want to do!" I yelled.

"Yeah, I guess you do" Sonnyboy said, as he slammed the three spoons down on the table, "like put another KING COBRA in my bed and embarrass me!"

"Well you embarrassed me first!" I said.

Sonnyboy scrunched his face and said, "that snake could have killed me!"

I laughed a little. Sonnyboy stopped rolling the flatware, folded his arms, pushed his head forward and bucked his eyes at me and said "Oh, so now you want to laugh at my pain?"

"Sonnyboy, that was a little old Gardner snake. It was harmless. It couldn't hurt nobody," I said as I shook out the napkin to re-roll the flatware.

Sonnyboy leaned into me with his big ears while tilting his head and said, "A snake is a snake and I don't like them!" He pushed out his lips and folded his arms in an angry huff.

I stopped rolling the flatware and said, "Well, I don't like it when you always messing with me and stuff! I told you before to leave me alone!"

Sonnyboy burst out, "So!" He turned back and started rolling the flatware again.

I turned to him again and said, "So, you should have left me alone! By the way, why do you pick on me so much, anyway?"

"Cause you always bossing everybody around!" He said.

"What!" I blurted.

"You always telling everybody what to do, Sustahgurl! Like you the queen or something," Sonnyboy smiled real big.

He took his hand and messed with my ponytails, "And you are not the boss of me little girl!"

I smacked his hands out of my head and said, "I'm not trying to be your boss, silly. I just wish you wouldn't pick on me so much!"

Sonnyboy chuckled and said, "You're still bossy."

I grinned real big and said, "Yeah, and you a cry-baby."

He stopped rolling the flatware, lost his grin and said, "Sustahgurl, that was not funny it was just plain mean! And you better tell Aunt Lena what you did."

"Well, if you knew I did it, why didn't you just tell Mother and Daddy?"

"Cause you would have told Aunt Lena that I put my foot in your sandwich. She had already spanked me for dropping those stink water bombs on Uncle Jack. So, I didn't say nothing. But you didn't have to lie or put that snake in my bed. As a matter of fact, why did you lie? You could have just told on me and I would have gotten in worse trouble than you," He said with a puzzled voice.

I looked at Sonnyboy, equally as puzzled, and said, "I don't know. I guess I was so mad that you and my brothers were laughing at me. I didn't tell because I didn't want Mother to feel sorry for you again and make me apologize.

And YES, I did have to put that snake in your bed 'cause you started it! And all ya'll were laughing at me! But, I guess you are right I do need to find a way to tell Mother the truth."

Sonnyboy tilted his head slightly and said, "Well, when my mama was living her favorite saying was, 'Trust God, do the right thing right now 'cause there is no time like the present.' You should tell Aunt Lena before she finds out from somebody else."

For once Sonnyboy was right and he even made sense. I didn't want one of my brothers to tell Mama the truth, but I still didn't want to tell Mama that I lied!

CHAPTER ELEVEN

It's another Saturday! Father took us on our special Saturday trip. We all went to the local candy store to get suckers. I love the sour apple suckers. I like the way they make my tongue tingle in the back. I always save my candy. I know my brothers will eat theirs all up and beg for mine. They will all beg for a lick, but I won't give it to them. I know it's wrong, I just like to do it. Father brought me back to the house and took all the boys to the ballpark. He works hard at the restaurant all week long, but he always makes time for us.

I ran in the house and found Mother sitting on the couch in the basement folding clothes. I flopped on the couch and said, "Hey Mother. Where's Peewee?"

Mother said, "She's taking a nap. Would you go and check on her please?"

"Yes Ma'am." I jumped up and put my sour apple sucker on the table.

I ran up the steps to check on Peewee as fast as I could to see if I could beat my fastest time. When I came back, I reported to Mother, "She's still sleep."

Mother said, "O.K., well help me finish folding these clothes then."

I huffed a little and turned up my face. Before picking up the first piece of clothing out of the basket, I reached to get my candy and it was gone! I didn't say anything. I just kept looking around the room, but I didn't see my candy any-where.

Mother was still sitting, folding the clothes and asked, "What are you looking for?"

I fumbled in my shirt pockets. I patted my pants. I looked under the table and finally said, "I had a green apple sucker Father bought me today. Have you seen it?"

Mother said "No, I didn't see it." I got up and started looking around the room.

I knew that I had put my sucker on the table, but maybe I had laid it down somewhere else and forgot.

I asked Mother again, "Mother, are you sure you didn't see my sucker that Father bought me?"

Mother answered, "No, but where did you put it?"

"I put it right here on this table." I whined.

Mother said, "Well let's finish the clothes then you can look for it."

After the clothes were finished, I searched for my sucker all over the house. I couldn't find it any-where. I went back to the family room with a su-per long face and flopped on the couch.

Mother was sitting on the couch doing a crossword puzzle.

"What's wrong with you?" She said.

"I can't find my candy." I whimpered and puffed my face.

She asked, "Well, where did you leave it last?"

"I told you Mother I put it right here on this table. Father bought us all a sucker today. He said we could eat them after dinner. Now everybody is going to have a sucker tonight and I won't have one."

I sulked and stared at the cartoons on the television totally not interested. Suddenly, I smelled the sweetest most delicious smell. It was a sour apple sucker. I turned and looked at Mother. She was sitting on the couch munching on my sucker!

My eyes popped wide open and I said, "Mother you lied to me! You said you didn't see my sucker."

Mother turned and twisted my sucker all around in her mouth and said, "Yes, I guess I did lie to you. Now, is there anything you want to tell me?" She questioned me with a very curious tone in her voice and her breathe smelled like sour apples.

I felt my stomach drop and knew that I should just go on and tell the truth.

I was so scared. I wasn't sure if Mother was going to be mad? Would she put me on punishment? I just sat there for a while and just looked at Mother with my hands pushed deep in my pockets. I shifted my eyes around in my head.

Mother took my sucker out of her mouth. With a sadness in her voice, she said, "I'm waiting Mary Ethel for an answer."

I stood up from the couch and looked Mother straight in the eye. I then took a deep breath and mumbled softly, "I put the snake in Sonnyboy's bed."

Mother frowned and said, "What did you say?"

I repeated louder, "I put the snake in Sonnyboy's bed."

"So why didn't you just tell me the truth? I asked you twice if you did it?" she scolded.

I answered softly, "I don't know."

Mother turned to me with a smile on her face and my sucker in her mouth, "I knew you did it. I just wanted you to tell me on your own. I talked to Miss Crystal and she came up with that Church School lesson. Even after that lesson, you still didn't come and tell me the truth. You just kept letting those lies keep rolling up. Now I know that Sonnyboy made you mad, but you could have told me what he did. And when I asked you for the truth, you should have told me the truth. You didn't have to lie. Nobody likes a liar."

I asked Mother hesitantly, "Are you going to spank me?"

"I should!" she said, as she gave me 'the face.'

"But I won't. However, you won't be eating your sucker with the rest of the kids after dinner. You are on punishment for all this week. Your sucker is now my sucker, and she crunched down on my sucker. However, you may be able to earn another one if you behave! And I have something special that you will be doing."

"Oh man…" I sighed

Mother brought two huge baskets of clothes to fold that included Sonnyboy's clothes.

"You will be folding them all on your own my sweet daughter."

I sighed again, "UGH.....Oh man....."

So there you have the whole story about me, Sustahgurl, and the Annoying Sonnyboy! Even though I told the truth, Mother still put me on punishment! Can you believe that? She said in the end I told the truth, but I should not have told her a lie. I did the wrong thing by taking my own revenge and lying to her. She made us both apologize to one another, and she made Sonnyboy vacuum for a week. He is still staying with us and he is still annoying! But he's still family!

And even though I know I was wrong for lying, I also learned it doesn't feel good to be lied to. I made up my mind; I am going to try my best to tell the truth!

So here is my first truth: I still grin when I think about THE ANNOYING SONNYBOY, smacking, hitting, jumping, skipping, and screaming all over my brothers room when he found that snake!